"Roscoe," **Emma said,** "I love Goofy. But he sits when you say *fetch*."

"And he lies down when you say *sit*," Gus added.

"Goofy can learn anything!" I said. "He could win that dog trick contest if he wanted to!"

My mouth said all that real fast.

While my brain was still trying to catch up.

I hate it when that happens.

Also by Katherine Applegate

The One and Only Ivan

The Roscoe Riley Rules series

#1: *Never Glue Your Friends to Chairs*

#2: *Never Swipe a Bully's Bear*

#3: *Don't Swap Your Sweater for a Dog*

#4: *Never Swim in Applesauce*

#5: *Don't Tap-Dance on Your Teacher*

#6: *Never Walk in Shoes That Talk*

#7: *Never Race a Runaway Pumpkin*

ROSCOE RILEY
RULES

 #3 Don't Swap Your
Sweater for a Dog

Katherine Applegate
illustrated by Brian Biggs

HARPER
An Imprint of HarperCollinsPublishers

For Julia and Jake,
with love

Roscoe Riley Rules #3: Don't Swap Your Sweater for a Dog
Text copyright © 2008 by Katherine Applegate
Illustrations copyright © 2008 by Brian Biggs

Library of Congress Cataloging-in-Publication Data
Applegate, Katherine.
   Don't swap your sweater for a dog / Katherine Applegate ; illustrated
by Brian Biggs. — 1st ed.
       p.   cm.
   ISBN 978-0-06-239250-3
   Summary: Determined to win a trophy of some kind, first-grader
Roscoe swaps a hand-knitted sweater from his grandmother for the
chance to enter his new neighbor's very clever dog in a trick contest.
   [1. Dogs—Training—Fiction. 2. Sweaters—Fiction. 3. Contests—
Fiction. 4. Schools—Fiction.] I. Humorous stories.
PZ7.A6483Don   2008   2007033409
[Fic]   CIP
                                                               AC

17 18 19 20   BVG   10 9 8 7 6 5 4 3 2
❖
Revised paperback edition, 2016

Don't Swap Your
Sweater For a Dog

Contents

1. Welcome to Time-Out.................... 1

2. Something You Should Know
   Before We Get Started.................... 3

3. Something Else You Should Know
   Before We Get Started.................... 5

4. The World's Best Roscoe Riley......... 6

5. The World's Ugliest Sweater............. 12

6. Jump, Frog, Jump!......................... 18

7. Pandas.. 27

8. Roscoe Riley, Superteacher............. 32

9. The Swap.................................... 42

10. The Toe-Tapping Trick................... 52

11. Truly Terrific Tricks...................... 60

12. MY Dog...................................... 71

13. The World's Best Backward
    Somersault Team.......................... 76

14. Good-Bye from Time-Out.............. 78

15. Roscoe's Time-Out Activities.......... 80

1

Welcome to Time-Out

Hey! Want to play?

Oops. I mean, want to play when I'm done with time-out?

I sort of kind of got in some trouble again.

'Cause I sort of kind of borrowed

somebody's dog.

I only borrowed him so I could win a trophy.

A shiny, sparkly, silver trophy.

You've probably borrowed a dog before, right?

A cat? A gerbil? A tarantula?

Oh. Well, I had my reasons.

It's a long story, actually.

Usually when I end up in time-out, there's a long story to tell.

And since you're here anyway, I'll bet you'd like to hear it. . . .

2

Something You Should Know
Before We Get Started

Just because your dog cannot read a book does not mean he isn't a winner.

Maybe he just hasn't figured out his real talent yet.

3

Something Else You Should Know
Before We Get Started

If your grandma knits you a sweater with pandas and smiley faces and hearts and baby ducks on it, do not give it to Martin.

Or anybody else.

It has sentimental value, you know.

4

The World's Best Roscoe Riley

This all started because my little sister won another trophy.

Hazel is still in preschool. And she already has a golden trophy from Little Minnows swim team. And one for being the Fastest Skipper in Ms. MacNamara's pre-K class.

So you can see why I was the teensiest bit annoyed when she came home with *another* trophy.

I'd had a long, hard day at school.

On account of an incident involving chocolate milk.

Did you know that if you blow through a straw into chocolate milk, the bubbles will volcano right out of your cup?

The bubbling part is way cool.

Cleaning up the mess afterward is not so cool.

Anyway, after all that, I didn't need to hear Hazel's big news as soon as I opened the door.

"Roscoe!" she screamed. "I wonned another one! For bestest sitting-stiller for the month at circle time!"

"I never got a trophy, and I sit still," I

said. "Well, sometimes I do."

Life is so not fair.

I dropped my backpack in the hall. I kicked off my tennis shoes. Then I flopped on the couch.

"You will not be getting any trophies for neatest boy on planet Earth," Mom said.

"Backpack in the closet. Shoes in your room." She kissed the top of my head.

"I want a trophy," I said in that whining voice you use when you feel really sorry for yourself.

"You got that little plastic statue in kindergarten last year," Mom said. "For most improved hand raising."

"I mean a *real* trophy," I said. "A big, heavy one. Made of gold."

"Shoes," Mom said. "Backpack."

I got off the couch and picked up my shoes and my backpack.

"You are the best burper in first grade," my big brother Max said.

He burped an extra loud one.

It was beautiful. Like music.

"But I'm still the best in the world," Max added.

Which is true. My brother has a gift.

"Everybody's got something cool like a trophy or a statue or something to take to show-and-tell," I said.

"*Every*body?" Mom asked.

"Last week Gus brought his yellow belt from karate," I said. "He got a little gold trophy cup with it. And today Emma brought her piano statue. She got it for practicing lots. It's of that grouchy guy."

"Ludwig van Beethoven," said Mom. "He was a famous music writer."

"Even you have a trophy, Mom," I said. "For selling Girl Scout cookies."

"That was a very long time ago," Mom said. "I was a great little salesperson, though. I could sell snow to a polar bear. I could sell water to an otter. I could sell—"

"Gee, Mom," I interrupted. "You are

big-time not helping me feel better. Which is sort of your job, after all."

Mom gave me a hug. "Sorry, sweetheart. You just be the very best Roscoe you can be. That's all that matters."

Easy for you to say, I thought. *You have a cookie trophy.*

Nobody gives a trophy for being The World's Best Roscoe Riley.

5

The World's Ugliest Sweater

"Don't forget Emma and Gus are coming over for a playdate," Mom said after I put my stuff away.

"Mom," I said with a groan, "we are not having a playdate. Hazel has playdates. We are hanging out."

"Well, when they get to the house for the

hang-out, please wear your new sweater if you go outside," Mom said.

"I will never wear that sweater," I said.

I crossed my arms over my chest. To show I meant business.

"Your grandmother knitted that sweater with her own two hands," Mom said.

"It has hearts on it! And flowers! And smiley faces! And baby ducks!" I cried.

"No sweater," Mom said, "no hang-out with Gus and Emma."

She tossed me the sweater. I put it on.

One side dangled down to my knees.

There was a pink bunny on the right sleeve. I hadn't noticed him before.

"NO!" Max cried. He covered his eyes. "Not the sweater of doom!"

Hazel wrinkled up her nose. "Why is there a monkey on the elbow?"

13

"That's a puppy," Mom said. She frowned. "At least, I think it is."

"Goofy and I are going to wait for Gus and Emma on the front porch," I said. "Cross your fingers nobody sees me."

"It was knit with love," Mom said. "It has sentimental value."

"What's mentisental value?" I asked.

"*Sentimental value* means you have to pretend to love your sweater when Grandma's here," Max said.

"*Sentimental value*," said Mom, "means that a gift is special to you because it came from someone you love."

I went outside. Goofy came with me.

He is a big, whitish guy dog with floppy ears.

His tail is usually in high gear.

And he almost always has something

in his mouth.

Right now he had Mom's cell phone.

"Not a good idea, Goofy," I said.

I went back inside and gave Mom the wet cell phone.

When I returned to the porch, Emma's dad dropped off Gus and Emma.

Gus and Emma live on the same street. It's a few blocks away from my house.

I wish I lived near them. Then we could be neighbors and best friends. Which is

very nice for hang-outs.

They ran over to the porch. Goofy licked their hands and wagged his tail extra speedy.

Then he licked one of Gus's sneakers for a while.

"You look kind of down in the dumps, Roscoe," Emma said.

"My sweater's ugly," I said. "And also I don't have any trophies and stuff like you guys."

Emma thought. "I would call your sweater interesting."

"I would call it very interesting," Gus said. "Why is there an armadillo on your shoulder?"

"That's a cow," I said.

"No," said Emma. "I'm pretty sure that's a kangaroo."

"COULD WE STOP TALKING ABOUT MY SWEATER?" I demanded.

Gus grinned. "Maybe you could get a blue ribbon for World's Weirdest Sweater."

I gave him my extra scary look.

"Okay, okay. No more sweater talk," he said.

"You know," said Emma, "it's never too late to get a trophy or a medal for something. You could learn to be a rodeo rider. Or an Olympic high diver."

Goofy started chasing his tail. He spun in crazy circles. He looked like a big white doughnut.

"Maybe Goofy could win a trophy for Best Tail Chaser," Gus said.

Goofy slammed into a bush.

"Or not," Emma added.

6

Jump, Frog, Jump!

We decided to play fetch with Goofy in the front yard.

We threw lots of tennis balls. Sometimes Goofy brought them back.

But mostly he just chewed them.

He even got three balls in his mouth at once.

He had a big, hairy clown smile.

When a boy walked by with his dog, Goofy ran over to say hello.

The dog was a little white poodle. He was wearing a silly doggie sweater with kitties on it.

"Sit, Edward," the boy said to the poodle.

Edward sat down. He did not move. He looked like a puffy statue.

Goofy raced around Edward in crazy circles. He barked. And sniffed.

And barked some more.

He looked goofy.

"I'm Martin," the boy said. "I just moved here a couple weeks ago. We used to live in Alaska."

"Did you live in one of those ice cube houses?" I asked.

"He means an igloo," Emma said.

Martin laughed. "Nope. Just a regular old house."

"Yeah," Gus said. "We live in regular old houses, too."

Martin pointed to my sweater. "Is that a poodle on your shoulder?"

"We're still trying to figure that out," I said.

"I really like animals," Martin said. "It's

a cool sweater."

I waited for him to laugh. But he didn't.

"I'm Roscoe," I said at last. "And that's Gus and Emma."

"Shake hands, Edward," Martin said.

Edward held up his paw.

Gus shook it. Emma shook it. I shook it.

Goofy licked it.

"Say hello, Edward," Martin said.

"Arf-arf," Edward said.

It was not exactly "hello," but you could tell what he meant.

"Wow! Your dog is amazing," said Emma.

"I was going to enter him in the Truly Terrific Trick Contest this weekend," Martin said. "But I have a tuba lesson."

"Do you mean the contest at the street

fair?" Emma asked. "I saw a poster for that. Kids and their dogs can enter. And the winner gets a trophy."

"A trophy?" I asked. "Really?"

"Do they have a prize for Stupidest Pet Trick?" Gus asked. "I'll bet Goof could win that one!"

Goofy lay on his back on the sidewalk.

I think he was ignoring Gus.

"What's your dog's name?" Martin asked.

"Goofy," I said. It sounded kind of lame next to a name like *Edward*.

Goofy wriggled on his back like a snake. His tongue was hanging out.

"What's he doing?" Martin asked.

"Itching," I said.

"Edward is never itchy," Martin said. He reached into his backpack. "Watch this."

Martin took out a book. "Just a regular book, right?" He showed it to me. "Now read it."

"I've already read that," I said.

"Not you," Martin said. "Edward."

I laughed. "Your dog cannot read!"

"Why not?" Martin asked.

"Because he is a dog," I said. I said it very slowly and clearly.

Since apparently Martin was a little crazy.

"Just watch," Martin said.

He put the book on the ground. It was called *Frog on a Log*.

"Open the book, Edward," said Martin.

Edward put his little white poodle paw on the book.

He pulled on the cover.

The book flipped open.

"Good dog, Edward," Martin said. "Now read to Roscoe."

Edward looked at the first page. So did I.

It said:

> Frog on a log
> in a big, dark bog.

Edward said:

> Arf arf arf arf
> arf arf arf arf arf.

"Good dog, Edward," said Martin. "Next page."

Edward turned the page with his nose. I looked over his shoulder.

The page had three words:

Jump, frog, jump!

Edward said:

Arf arf arf!

I looked at Martin.
I looked at Edward.

He didn't look so silly anymore. Even with the kitty sweater.

"That dog is a genius," I said.

We looked at Goofy.

He was eating an old gym sock.

"Your dog is nice too," Martin said.

7

Pandas

I thought about Edward and that book all the next day.

Especially when it was reading time.

Gus and Emma and I are in the same reading group. There are six kids.

All the groups have animal names. There are Panthers. Giraffes. And Tigers.

Gus and Emma and I are Pandas.

We each read two pages out loud.

When someone else is reading, we have to follow the rules:

1. No talking.
2. No laughing if somebody makes a mistake.
3. No sound effects.

Ms. Diz made up the third rule after we read our last book.

It was called *Honk! Honk! Beep! Beep!*

When we were all done, I asked Ms. Diz a question. I'd been wondering about it ever since meeting Edward.

"Ms. Diz," I asked, "do you think a dog can read?"

Ms. Diz thought for a second.

"Well, I doubt it, Roscoe," she said.

"Why do you ask?"

"Because Gus and Emma and me met a dog who could read *Frog on a Log*."

"He wasn't exactly reading, Roscoe," Gus said. "It was more like weird barking."

"But he barked when there was an actual word," I said. "If we can learn to read, why can't a dog?"

"Well, Roscoe," Ms. Diz said, "it's not that simple. Before you can read, you need to know your letters and the sounds they make. I've never met a dog who could do that."

"I'm telling you, Edward was reading," I said.

Sometimes, even when I'm not for-sure right, I kind of get stuck acting like I'm right.

I was feeling a little bit sticky at the moment.

Even Gus didn't think Edward was a reader.

And Gus believes everything.

I mean, Gus believes toads give you warts.

And everybody knows that's not true.

Toads are great.

Frogs give you warts.

"I'll bet you dogs can read," I said. "I'll bet I could teach Goofy."

"Roscoe," Emma said, "I love Goofy. But he sits when you say *fetch*."

"And he lies down when you say *sit*," Gus added.

I know they weren't trying to be mean.

But I felt like I had to defend my dog.

"Goofy can learn anything!" I said. "He could win that dog trick contest if he wanted to!"

My mouth said all that real fast.

While my brain was still trying to catch up.

I hate it when that happens.

8

Roscoe Riley, Superteacher

Maybe you think it's easy being a teacher.

I used to.

After all, they get to boss around little kids all day.

How hard could that be?

Well, here are some things you should know in case you ever become a teacher:

1. Do not grouch at your students. Even if they stop their learning so they can chew their tail.

2. Do not try to make them learn everything in one day.

   On account of their brain might explode.

   Or they might take a nap.

3. Don't forget to praise your students when they do something right.

   A treat is a good idea.

   A cookie for the teacher is always nice, too.

I might even have given up teaching when my student tried to eat a book.

That can be pretty hard on a teacher.

But I kept seeing a beautiful picture in my head.

It was me at the dog trick contest. With Goofy by my side.

And a judge handing me a gigantic trophy.

The contest was Saturday. And today was Wednesday.

I didn't have a lot of time to teach Goofy to read like Edward.

The first thing I had to do was find the right book for Goofy.

I let him come with me to my bedroom. In case there was a book he especially liked.

For example, I like to read about dinosaurs. Also superheroes.

I found some books about dogs. (Because Goofy is one.)

And cars. (Because he likes to ride in them.)

And cats. (Because he likes to chase them.)

I put them on the floor in front of Goofy.

"Which one do you like, Goof?" I asked.

He didn't answer.

He was sniffing a dirty shirt on the floor. It had a nice, tasty spot of dried spaghetti sauce on it.

I picked a book called *Bad Cat Goes to the Vet*.

I figured Goofy would get a kick out of that.

We went to the kitchen. I stuffed my pockets with dog treats. And grabbed a banana for me.

"Where are you two going?" Mom asked.

"I'm teaching Goof to read," I said.

"After that, could you teach him to do

the dishes?" she asked.

As soon as we got outside, Goofy saw Hector.

Hector is a squirrel who lives in a big oak tree behind our house.

He loves to tease poor old Goofy.

Hector made some "Come and get me, doggie!" sounds.

Goofy flew across the yard.

His ears were flapping. His tongue was flapping.

Hector waited.

And waited.

And waited.

When Goofy was just a couple feet away, Hector zipped up his tree.

He made some more noises that said, "You moron! Why don't you ever learn, dogface?"

Goofy stared up at him, panting.

"You almost had him this time, guy," I said.

I always tell him that.

I went over to the other side of the yard. Away from Hector.

That's another thing about teaching.

It's hard to get anything done if your

student is busy trying to eat a squirrel.

"Goofy!" I called. I peeled my banana. "Come! Time to read."

Goofy saw the banana.

I forgot how much that guy loves fruit.

He dashed across the yard.

He leaped up into my arms. I fell backward.

And we just kept rolling.

And rolling.

And rolling.

Man, was that fun!

We lay on the ground. Goofy licked my face.

I gave him the whole banana.

While he ate, I grabbed my book about Bad Cat.

"Today we are going to learn to read," I said. "First I will go."

I read nice and slow:

> Bad Cat chases Big Rat.
> Big Rat chases Bad Cat.
> Poor Bad Cat!
> Big Rat bit his tail.
> Bad Cat must go to the vet.

"Your turn," I said.

Goofy tried to eat the banana peel.

He looked at me with his big, happy eyes.

I could tell he wanted to understand.

But he couldn't quite figure me out.

I remembered feeling that way when I first learned to read.

Ms. Diz would point to a word like DOG.

And all I would see was ♣✭◇.

So I knew how Goofy felt.

I gave him a nice ear-scratch.

"We'll try again tomorrow, Goof," I said.

But he wasn't listening.

Hector was back.

9

The Swap

For the rest of the week, I worked with Goofy.

He did not learn any letters.

Or any words.

None.

But we had fun chasing Hector and rolling around together.

Even though it had nothing to do with reading.

On Friday I sat on the front steps with Goofy.

I had on my Grandma sweater. Because Mom made me wear it. Again.

Mom was mulching the garden.

Mulch is kind of like dirt. Mom says when she puts it around the plants, it's like giving them a blanket.

But if you ask me, a blanket shouldn't smell like cow poop.

"Why aren't you and Goofy working?" Mom asked.

"The trick contest is tomorrow," I said. "And he still hasn't learned anything." I sighed. "I think maybe Goofy is a dummy, Mom."

I whispered that last part so he wouldn't hear me.

"Roscoe, Goofy is the best dog in the

world," Mom said. "But he's just a dog. He can only do doggie things. If you work hard with him, maybe he can learn to fetch or shake hands. But mostly he's going to do what he does best—love you!"

"But he doesn't even know one letter, Mom!" I said.

Mom shook her head. "Maybe the problem isn't the student," she said. "Maybe the problem is the teacher."

"But I'm a good teacher!" I cried.

"That poodle you told me about—" Mom said.

"Edward."

"Edward," Mom said. "Edward wasn't reading, sweetie. It's just a trick his owner taught him. A good trick, but still a trick." Mom stood up. "I'm going to the garage to get some more mulch. I'll be right back."

I pictured that trophy. Shiny. Heavy. Gold.

If Goofy weren't so goofy, I could have that trophy.

Down the sidewalk I saw Martin and Edward. Martin waved.

He paused and said something to Edward.

Edward waved his little poodle paw at me.

Goofy ran over to say hello.

The old-fashioned dog way.

With major sniffing and tail wagging.

"Hey," I said. I gave Edward a pat.

Today he was wearing a pink-and-green sweater.

"Is that a white tiger on your sweater?" Martin asked.

"It's a panda," I said.

"It's like you've got a whole zoo on there," Martin said.

"Hey, how did you teach Edward to read?" I asked.

Martin just shrugged. "It's kind of a secret," he said.

"I'm trying to teach Goofy so he can be in the trick contest," I said. "But he's not a very good student."

Goofy licked my hand.

I felt awful for saying that about a friend.

"Don't get me wrong," I added. "He's the greatest. He just doesn't know his letters."

"Well," Martin said, "even Edward took a long time to learn."

"I wish I could take Edward to the contest," I said. "He'd for sure win."

Goofy sighed and lay down on the sidewalk.

I felt even worse.

Martin thought for a minute. Then he started grinning.

"You know," he said, "I might be able to let you borrow Edward."

I felt my eyes get wide. "You would let me borrow Edward for the contest?" I cried. "Name your price!"

Martin thought. "You know, I do like that sweater. It's very unusual."

I had to think for a minute. "You mean *this* sweater? This one I'm wearing? With smiley faces and monkeys on it?"

"Yep," said Martin. "It's one of a kind."

"That's for sure," I agreed. "But the thing is, my grandma knitted this for me. With love."

47

Martin shrugged. "That's okay. It was just an idea."

I pictured myself holding that shiny, glittering-in-the-sun, could-even-be-real-gold trophy.

I looked down at poor old goofy Goofy.

I checked over my shoulder.

Mom was back in the garden, busy mulching.

"No, wait," I whispered. "It's a deal. Follow me."

We went behind some tall bushes. Goofy and Edward came, too.

I took off my itchy, ugly sweater.

It was the best trade I'd ever made.

Except for the time I talked Hazel into giving me her double-scoop chocolate-chip-cookie-dough ice cream cone for a pink rubber band.

"Don't put it on till you get to the end of the street, okay?" I said.

Martin held up the sweater. "Is that a crocodile?" he asked.

"I think it's a rabbit," I said.

I touched the crocodile-rabbit's little nose.

"My tuba lesson is at ten tomorrow," Martin said. "I'll drop off Edward before I go."

"Great!" I said. "Ed, give me five!"

Edward put up his paw and we high-fived.

"It's Edward," Martin said. "Not Ed."

I'm not sure, but I think maybe Goofy groaned.

Goofy and I went back to the porch. I was cold.

On account of I didn't have my sweater anymore.

It was ugly and itchy. But it sure was warm.

"Roscoe," Mom said, "where's your sweater?"

"I—" I swallowed. "I, uh, took it off."

Which was true.

True-ish.

"It's chilly out here," Mom said. "You really need it."

"Goof and I are going in now, anyway," I said. "I think he's had enough learning. See you, Mom."

Goofy and I ran inside. I closed the door behind me.

In the hallway was a picture of me and Max and Hazel and my grandma and grandpa at a baseball game.

I thought about Grandma knitting all those furry little animals and smiley faces.

It probably took her a very long time.

She'd made that panda special. Because I was in the Panda reading group.

Martin would never even know that.

10

The Toe-Tapping Trick

It was warm and sunny on Saturday morning.

That was a good thing.

Because I didn't need to wear my sweater.

And because when Martin brought Edward over, Martin wasn't wearing my sweater.

His sweater, I mean.

"I'll pick Edward up after my tuba lesson," Martin said.

I took Edward's leash.

"Hey, did you know that sweater has 'I love you' written on the right sleeve in teensy yellow letters?" Martin asked.

"No," I said quietly.

"And I found a mouse and a raccoon on it," Martin said.

"That's not a mouse," I said. "It's a possum. My grandma and grandpa have a possum family living in their backyard."

"It's a great sweater," Martin said. "I wish Edward had one so we could match."

Today Edward was wearing a green T-shirt. It said "World's Smartest Dog" on it.

"Almost forgot," Martin said. He pulled

Frog on a Log out of his backpack.

"That's okay," I said. "I have a book he'll like even better. It's Goofy's favorite. *Bad Cat Goes to the Vet*."

"Well, there's something I need to tell you," Martin said. He made a throat noise. "See, Edward can't exactly read."

"What do you mean?" I asked.

What about my trophy? I was thinking.

"It's a trick. I just signal him how many times to bark," Martin said. "I count the words on a page. Then I tap my foot. If it says, 'Jump, frog, jump!' then I tap my foot three times. And Edward barks three times."

"So it only looks like he's reading," I said. "Oh."

I was disappointed.

I sort of liked believing dogs could read.

Also I could see how I'd been a little hard on Goofy.

"You'd better stick with *Frog on a Log* since Edward is used to it. It's a cool trick," Martin said. "I'm sure you guys will win."

Martin patted Edward's poodle pom-pom. "Be sure he gets plenty of water," he said. "He likes springwater. Cold. But not too cold."

"Goofy likes toilet water," I said. "He's very open-minded."

"He's a nice dog," Martin said.

Goofy licked Edward. Then he licked Martin. Then he licked me.

"Yes," I said. "He really is."

. . .

Dad drove me and Edward to the contest.

I'd told him and Mom a teensy little fib about why I was taking Edward instead of Goofy.

I said Martin had to go to his tuba lesson. So he couldn't take Edward to the contest.

Which was true.

Then I said I was doing Martin a favor. Because he really wanted Edward in the show, so he asked me to help out.

That part was not so true.

Mom and Max and Hazel were coming to the show later. But I had to get there early to sign up.

"I'll say this for you, Edward," Dad said as we parked. "You sure smell better than Goofy."

"I think he's wearing doggie perfume, Dad," I said.

The contest was in a park by the street fair. Dogs and kids were everywhere.

We walked over to a long table covered with paper and pencils. Dad helped me fill out a form so I could enter the contest.

A lady gave me a number to pin to my shirt. It was 13.

"Thirteen is not very lucky," I said.

"Could be your lucky number today," the lady said. "What's your dog's name?"

I started to say, "He's not my dog."

But instead I just said, "Edward."

As we walked toward the big field, Dad said, "Goofy looked a little forlorn as we drove away."

"What's *forlorn*?" I asked.

"It's how you feel when you think your boy doesn't like you anymore."

"Goofy couldn't win a trophy, Dad," I said.

As soon as I said it, I felt bad. Even though it was the truth.

"He could win for biggest appetite," Dad joked.

He gave me a hug. Then he patted Edward.

"Good luck, guys," he said. "We'll meet you after the contest. I'm going to go save some seats so we have a good view. See ya, Ed."

"It's Edward," I said.

"Figures," said Dad.

11

Truly Terrific
Tricks

The dogs and their kids lined up in a
special area.

The crowd got bigger.

I saw Gus and Emma. They waved.

I saw Mom and Hazel and Max.

They waved too.

Then I saw somebody else.

Goofy.

He wagged his tail and pulled on the leash Max was holding.

He barked hello.

I felt like I was on a playdate with the wrong friend.

I mean a *hang-out*.

Three judges sat in chairs behind a table. They had paper and pens and serious faces.

"Contestant number one," said a man on a loudspeaker. "Mary Lou Oliver and her dog, Moe."

Mary Lou and Moe went to the center of the field.

Moe rolled over. Then he played dead.

Next came Nico and Spinner. Spinner danced on his hind legs.

Noodles caught a Frisbee in midair.

Linus played a toy piano with his nose.

He was extra good.

But nobody was as good as Edward.

On the judges' table I could see lots of colored ribbons.

And one beautiful trophy.

It was silver. Not gold.

And smallish. Not huge.

But still, it was going to look great on my dresser.

And be a cool show-and-tell.

When other kids brought their ribbons and certificates and awards, I would have something to show at last.

More dogs did tricks.

My favorite was Astro. He chewed up a kid's homework for his trick.

On purpose.

But even that amazing trick couldn't

beat Edward's.

At last they called us.

"Roscoe Riley and his dog, Edward," the loudspeaker man said.

We walked onto the field. I turned toward the judges.

"Edward, the amazing reading dog, will now read from this book," I said.

The crowd made a "wow" noise.

The judges leaned forward.

I brought the book over so they could see the first page of *Frog on a Log*.

Then I took it back to Edward. I put the book in front of him.

"Open the book, Edward," I said.

Edward opened the book with his nose.

Just like I knew he would.

"Now read to us!" I said.

The first words in the story were "Frog on a log."

I tapped my foot four times. Just a little, so that only Edward could see.

He barked four times.

Just like I knew he would.

"He's right!" one of the judges exclaimed.

The crowd cheered.

And I knew right then that trophy was mine.

. . .

While we waited for the judges to make their decision, I went over to the stands to say hello to my family and Gus and Emma.

"You rocked!" Gus exclaimed. "You for-sure are going to win!"

"Not bad," Dad said, "for a dog who

wears perfume."

People crowded around me. Everyone wanted to pat Edward.

"How did you teach him to do that?" a man asked.

"How long have you owned him?" a lady asked.

"Why is he wearing a T-shirt?" a boy asked.

I tried to answer all the questions. But it felt a little funny.

On account of I had to pretend I knew the answers. Like I really was Edward's owner.

"Do you have any other pets?" a little girl asked.

At least I knew the answer to that one.

"I have a dog named Goofy," I said. "He's over there."

I pointed. Goofy was sitting by Max's feet. He looked sort of left out.

Maybe even forlorn.

"Can Goofy do cool tricks, too?" the little girl asked.

"Well, not exactly," I said. "He's still

learning. But he's a really great guy."

"Ladies and gentlemen!" the loudspeaker man said. "It is time for the awarding of prizes. If your name is called, please come to the judges' table to accept your award."

One of the judges stood up. She held a microphone in one hand and ribbons in the other.

"I just want to say that it was very difficult to determine a winner in this year's contest. What we especially love seeing is the wonderful bonds between dogs and their owners. A dog learns best when he is loved and praised. And it's clear that all these dogs are very much loved."

I looked down at Edward.

He was standing perfectly still.

I looked over at Goofy.

He was trying to catch a fly in his mouth.

"Third prize goes to Linus and Larry Dunn!" the judge announced.

Everyone clapped. Larry ran over with Linus to accept a yellow ribbon.

"Second prize goes to Astro and Penelope Watson," the judge said. "But don't you dare use that trick to get out of doing your homework!"

Finally, my moment arrived.

"And our first-prize trophy goes to the amazing team of Roscoe Riley and his dog, Edward!"

It was just like I'd imagined it.

Applause.

Cheering.

Even some barking.

We dashed over to the judges.

The trophy wasn't as heavy as I thought.

In fact, I think maybe it was plastic.

But it was a silver trophy, and it was mine.

12

MY Dog

I held the trophy high in the air. Edward and I ran across the field to my family.

There was lots of back patting.

And high-fiving.

And way-to-going.

I felt pretty amazing. I was definitely going to be the star of show-and-tell.

Something cold touched my hand.

I looked down, and there was Goofy.

He was nudging me with his nose.

He wagged his tail like he was happy for me.

He even touched noses with Edward.

Good old Goofy.

I gave him a hug.

"Will the contestants please return to the judges' table for photographs?" said the loudspeaker guy.

"Come on, Edward," I said. "They want to take our picture."

Edward and I walked back to the judges.

"Sit, Edward," I said. And of course Edward sat.

"Congratulations, Roscoe," the lady judge said. "You and Edward must have a very special relationship."

"Well, I—," I began. "He's a nice dog, yeah."

I looked back at my family.

Goofy was watching me. He wagged his tail. Just a little.

I held up the trophy. It glittered in the sun.

Just like I'd imagined.

Then I set the trophy down on the table.

"Edward's a nice dog," I said, "but he's not *my* dog."

"What do you mean, son?" another judge asked.

"That's my dog," I said. "Over there. I just borrowed Edward because I wanted a trophy, but he's not mine, he's Martin's, and I really want my sweater back too."

The judges just looked at me.

"What sweater, sweetheart?" asked the

lady judge finally. "I'm afraid you've lost us. And which dog is really your dog?"

I handed her Edward's leash. "I'll show you," I said.

"Goofy!" I called. "Goofy! Come here, boy!"

Goofy yanked free of Max. He dashed across the field like he was going after Hector.

He leaped into my arms.

We fell back.

We rolled and rolled and rolled and rolled.

It was great.

Goofy licked my nose.

The crowd went wild.

"This," I said, "is MY dog."

13

The World's Best Backward Somersault Team

They gave the trophy to the homework-eating dog instead.

But Goofy and I got a special white ribbon.

On the bottom, one of the judges wrote WORLD'S BEST BACKWARD SOMERSAULT TEAM.

When Martin came to pick up Edward, I told him the whole story.

I also told him I was really sorry, but I wanted my sweater back.

I told him I would pay him my allowance for as long as it took.

Martin said that was okay. Because even though he liked the sweater, it was awfully itchy.

14

Good-Bye from Time-Out

When I told my mom and dad about trading Grandma's sweater for Edward, they were not happy.

They were also not happy about the part where I fibbed about Martin wanting me to enter Edward in the contest. Although they were proud of me for telling them the truth eventually.

Also, for telling the judges the truth.

They said I was getting very mature.

So I asked, Does that mean no more time-outs?

Here I am. So I guess you can tell what their answer was.

It felt good to get Grandma's sweater back. In fact, I'm wearing it right now. I found a baby turtle and a worm on it while I've been sitting here.

It really is a work of art.

Too bad it's so itchy.

I don't even mind being in time-out so much today.

'Cause Goofy's here with me.

He got sent to time-out, too.

Something about eating the hot dogs we were going to have for dinner.

Good old Goofy.

RoScoE's

Time-Out
Activities!

10 BOOKS I THINK DOGS WOULD LIKE TO READ

by Me, Roscoe Riley

1. Tomcats in Time-Out:
   A Picture Book

2. The Amazing True Story of
   the Dog Who Ate an Entire
   Ham and Nobody Even Noticed

3. Doorknobs: A How-To Manual

4. The No Good, Very Bad Bathtub

5. The Cat in the Vat

6. Who Chewed the New Shoe?
Poems for Doggies

7. Little Puppy's Scratch-
and-Sniff Garbage Can

8. Fleas: The Unseen Enemy

9. Why People Don't Catch
Frisbees in Their Mouths,
and Other Questions about
Your Owner

10. Learn to Read in
Ten Easy Lessons!

10 MORE RULES TO LIVE BY

by Me, Roscoe Riley

#15 – Don't let your dog pull you on your bike.

#72 – Never fall asleep on a trampoline.

#36 – Don't trade your backpack for a sandwich.

#27 – Never bring dirt in your room, even if you want to grow grass.

#84 – Don't try to eat all the cookies in one sitting.

#55 - Never tickle your dad when he's asleep.

#49 - Don't leave your stuffed animals in the yard overnight.

#68 - Never taste your mom's lotion, even if it smells like candy.

#91 - Don't put raisins in your brother's bed.

#52 - Never cut your dog's hair.

CAN YOU SPOT THE DIFFERENCE?

If you want to stay out of trouble, you need to be able to tell when something's wrong. Try to find the seven things that have changed between these pictures.

DID YOU FIND THEM ALL?

Stuck in time-out again! What went wrong this time?
Read all about my next adventure in

RoSCoE RiLEY RULES

#4 Never Swim in
Applesauce

1

Welcome to Time-Out

Yep. It's me. Roscoe Riley.

Stuck in time-out again.

And speaking of stuck, have I got a story for you!

A very sticky story.

See, my class went on a field trip to an apple farm.

A field trip is when you go somewhere

more fun than even recess and lunch put together.

We went to an apple farm so we could learn about where our food comes from.

Besides the pizza delivery guy.

All the kids went. And our teacher.

And some moms and dads to make sure we didn't get rowdy or do trouble-making.

I didn't get rowdy.

Well, maybe just once or twice.

But I *did* get into a teeny, tiny, practically invisible bit of trouble.

Who knew there was a rule about not jumping into a giant tub of applesauce?

I'll bet you've done some applesauce swimming, haven't you?

No?

Well, trust me on this. You should stick

to swimming in real, live swimming pools.

Applesauce is very . . . well, appley.

But maybe I should start at the beginning.

The part before I got apple-slimed.

2

Something You Should Know
Before We Get Started

Worms are good for fishing and for scaring little sisters and sometimes dads.

But they do not make a very good snack.

I hear they taste sort of like mushy macaroni.

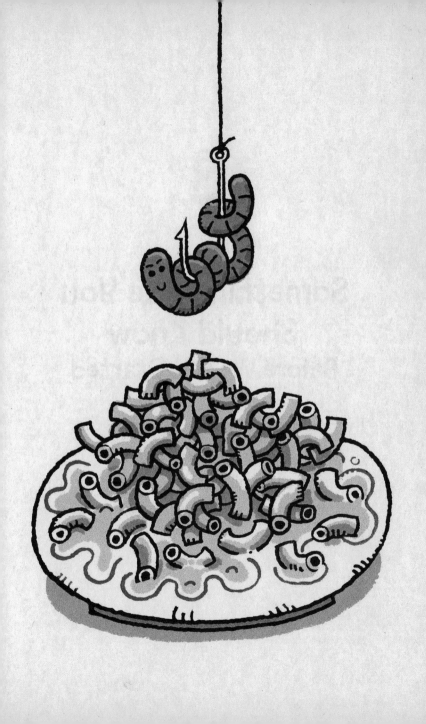

3

Something Else You Should Know
Before We Get Started

Everybody loves plain applesauce.

And cinnamon applesauce.

And even raspberry-flavored applesauce.

But boy-flavored applesauce?

Not so much.

4

Happy Apple Orchard

When I first heard about our field trip, I was pretty excited.

Almost as excited as my teacher, Ms. Diz.

She told us about the trip in a very thrilled way, with tons of exclamation points in her voice.

"Children!" Ms. Diz said first thing that morning. "I have a wonderful surprise! This

Friday we are going on a field trip! The first one for our class!" She grinned. "And the first one for me since I became a teacher!"

Ms. Diz is a brand-new teacher. I help her out whenever I can.

I know a lot because I am a retired kindergartner.

"My brother's class went on a trip to a bakery and they got free doughnuts," I said.

Then I raised my hand real quick because sometimes I forget to remember that part.

You aren't supposed to talk until you put your hand up in the air and wave it like crazy because that is better than just yelling at the top of your lungs.

"If we can't go on a bakery field trip, maybe a cotton-candy factory would be good. Or an aquarium with giant, kid-eating sharks," I added.

Sometimes my imagination button gets stuck on fast-forward.

"Those are great suggestions, Roscoe," said Ms. Diz. "But we've already made plans for this trip. I'll give you a hint, class. What have we been learning about the past few weeks?"

"If you squeeze your juice box hard, you get a gusher!" said Dewan.

"Do not pick your nose during snack time," Coco said.

For some reason, she looked right at me.

"The pencil sharpener is not for crayons," Gus offered.

Ms. Diz held up her hands to make a *T*. Like a coach taking a time-out.

She does that when she wants us to be

quiet. Which is pretty often, come to think of it.

"We've been learning about *where our food comes from*," Ms. Diz reminded us.

She said the last part very slowly. So our brains could catch up with her mouth.

"Remember we talked about how vegetables and fruits come from farms?" Ms. Diz asked. "And about how the farmers grow the food and pick it, then send it on trucks to stores where we can buy it? I know how much you guys love applesauce, and apple pies, and taffy apples," Ms. Diz said. "That's why we are going to visit—"

I finished for her. "THE GROCERY STORE!!!" I yelled. "I LOVE the grocery store because I push the cart for my mom and dad except not anymore because I knocked over a watermelon pile and that knocked over a lemon pile and whoa, that was cool because it looked just like pink lemonade!"

"Roscoe," said Ms. Diz while I stopped

to take a breath, "I need you to think before speaking. Okay?"

I thought for a while. "Okay!" I said after I figured I'd been thinking long enough.

"As I was trying to say," said Ms. Diz, "we are going to an apple orchard!"

"You mean where they make apples?" Gus asked.

"They don't *make* apples, they *grow* them," said Ms. Diz. "There are hundreds of apple trees at Happy Apple Orchard. They produce all kinds of apples. Green and red and yellow, sweet and sour. We'll each get to pick our own apples!"

That was way better than a field trip to a plain old field!

We did a lot of cheering and jumping out of our chairs and clapping.

Until Ms. Diz had to ring her gong.

It is a very loud bell that helps us Stay Focused.

Staying Focused is when you Stop Acting Like Preschoolers, Class.

"They make lots of food at Happy Apple too," Ms. Diz said when we were quiet. "We'll get to see them bake apple pies and make applesauce. We might even get to *eat* some! But only if you all are on your best behavior."

Pie and applesauce? That was too much great news.

Ms. Diz had to gong four times before we settled down.

But who could blame us?

We were going on a field trip to see happy apples!

Turn the page for a super-special look at
The One and Only Ivan, winner of the Newbery Medal
and a #1 *New York Times* bestseller!

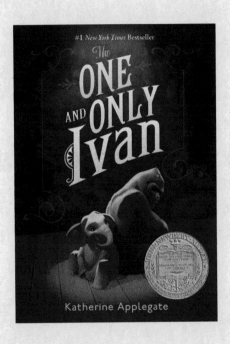

hello

I am Ivan. I am a gorilla.

It's not as easy as it looks.

names

People call me the Freeway Gorilla. The Ape at Exit 8. The One and Only Ivan, Mighty Silverback.

The names are mine, but they're not me. I am Ivan, just Ivan, only Ivan.

Humans waste words. They toss them like banana peels and leave them to rot.

Everyone knows the peels are the best part.

I suppose you think gorillas can't understand you. Of course, you also probably think we can't walk upright.

Try knuckle walking for an hour. You tell me: Which way is more fun?

I've learned to understand human words over the years, but understanding human speech is not the same as understanding humans.

Humans speak too much. They chatter like chimps, crowding the world with their noise even when they have nothing to say.

It took me some time to recognize all those human sounds, to weave words into things. But I was patient.

Patient is a useful way to be when you're an ape.

Gorillas are as patient as stones. Humans, not so much.

how I look

I used to be a wild gorilla, and I still look the part.

I have a gorilla's shy gaze, a gorilla's sly smile. I wear a snowy saddle of fur, the uniform of a silverback. When the sun warms my back, I cast a gorilla's majestic shadow.

In my size humans see a test of themselves. They hear fighting words on the wind, when all I'm thinking is how the late-day sun reminds me of a ripe nectarine.

I'm mightier than any human, four hundred pounds of pure power. My body looks made for battle. My arms, outstretched, span taller than the tallest human.

My family tree spreads wide as well. I am a great ape, and you are a great ape, and so are chimpanzees and orangutans and bonobos, all of us distant and distrustful cousins.

I know this is troubling.

I too find it hard to believe there is a connection across time and space, linking me to a race of ill-mannered clowns.

Chimps. There's no excuse for them.

Discover the unforgettable Newbery Medal–winning novel

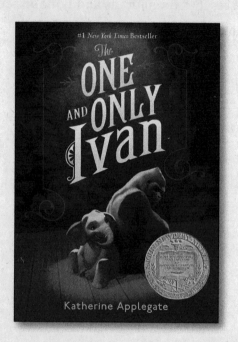

The One and Only Ivan is an uplifting story that celebrates the power of unexpected friendships, told through the eyes of a captive gorilla known as Ivan.

Don't miss the full-color collector's edition of *The One and Only Ivan!*